AF480639

The Color of Our Names

A Novella

Mahitab Mahmoud

Also By Mahitab Mahmoud

When Silence Shatters: A Collection of Short Stories

Praise for *When Silence Shatters:*

A Collection of Short Stories

"Mahmoud spins tales of injustice in Egypt in this collection of short stories."

— *Kirkus Reviews*

"Mahmoud's observation of gesture, dialogue, and the importance of ordinary moments makes every story sing."

— *Jamie Michele, Readers' Favorite*

"Each of these short narratives packs a punch and leaves you with something to ponder."

— *Pikasho Deka, Readers' Favorite*

Hardcover ISBN: 979-8-9949748-0-3

Paperback ISBN: 979-8-9949748-2-7

eBook ISBN: 979-8-9949748-1-0

Dedication

To everyone who has ever loved in silence,

lived in fear of being outed,

or carried two names in one heart.

Love is what brings us together.

Love is what sets us free.

Love wins.

Acknowledgments

To Sherine—

the light that never fades,

the peace I take refuge in while fighting my wars.

Contents

Author's Note

If you grew up in a society where your identity is hidden or unwelcome, you know what it means to carry two names—two worlds, two selves. One allows you to exist quietly under the radar; the other threatens your very existence if revealed.

If you did not grow up in such a society, this book invites you to imagine what that means—to whisper rather than speak, to glimpse the daily negotiations, the unspoken risks, and the price of simply being. The cost of identifying as LGBTQ+. The fear of being outed. The silence that becomes your oldest friend. The way your very existence becomes an act of rebellion, a silent one.

The Color of Our Names is for those who live unseen, and for those who are willing to see. The characters show you what it means to live a double life so convincingly that, one day, you forget which version of yourself is real.

—Mahitab Mahmoud

Fareed—One

Like every morning, Fareed wakes at 3 am before anyone else in the household because it's the only time he can have the room to himself without interruptions. He brews a cup of Turkish coffee in silence, tiptoeing around the kitchen so his family won't hear him. The rich aroma fills the small apartment as he returns to his room and logs into his social-media accounts.

Sleem, his youngest brother, sleeps soundly in the single bed across from him. Around them, the same album posters that once covered Fareed's childhood walls still cling stubbornly to the fading wallpaper—Amr Diab's 1994 *We Yloumouni* (Let them Blame Me), Ehab Tawfik's 1995 *Adda El Leil* (The Night has Passed), Latifa's 1998 *Taloomoni El Donya* (The World Blames Me), NSYNC's 1997 *No Strings Attached*, Backstreet Boys' 1999 *Millennium*, and Boyzone's 1998 *Where We Belong*.

The furniture in the bedroom is pure retro, not by design but by default. Every chair, every drawer, has outlived fashion and maybe hope itself. It's the same they've had since Fareed was born, heavy with memories, dust and the same stale smell as if time itself refuses to move on in this room.

Whenever Fareed and Sleem ask their father, Zakareya, to update the furniture, they hear the same response. "You know how expensive the furniture was? It's all Italian from Damietta. They don't make furniture like this anymore."

Fareed replies in his mind: *of course not. I'm sure the Italians would be surprised it survived almost five decades!*

"You don't understand its value," continues Zakareya, turning to their mother. "They don't understand, *ya* Amina."

"They don't," she echoes, pressing her lips together and shaking her head in slow motion—that familiar signal that means, *I told you not to bring this up. At least not now.*

Even their computer is a relic—first they had the 2004 model their father bought when he was promoted to senior accountant at Alexandria University. It lasted until Fareed saved up and replaced it with a 2011 upgrade—the one he got just before the Egyptian Uprising, the once-called *Arab Spring*. It was a year of pride and shame, of glory and pain, of hope and disappointment, of peace, war, and bloodshed. Fareed, like many Millennials who rallied against tyranny, despotism and poverty, refuses to recall what followed the interim government's promises, the televised speeches, the supposedly democratic elections.

He returns to his cup of coffee. He's about to get up and brew a second one when his phone screen lights up. A message from Eddie. Fareed glances at Sleem to make sure he's still asleep, then checks that the door is firmly shut.

Hello, early bird, types Eddie.

Good morning, sunshine, replies Fareed.

Did you get enough sleep?

You know I'm not a big fan of sleep. To me, it's just nap time… a way to recharge for the rest of the day.

Fareed, what did you say your name means again?

Unique.

Aha. So true…

Fareed smiles at his screen.

So, when will you move out? I just don't get how you're thirty-four and still live with your parents…

Fareed's smile fades.

Well, that's how it is here… You live with your parents until you can afford to get married or get paid well enough to rent an apartment in another city. I'm still looking for jobs in Cairo, but it's not that easy. My parents won't let me move out until one or the other happens.

You said they "won't" let you? Seriously?

Fareed hears the familiar creak of the wooden floor outside his room. That's his warning bell. His heart pounds. He quickly locks his phone screen and opens the Business Administration book on his desk. A soft knock follows. Amina pushes the door open just enough to peck inside.

"*Habibi yabni.* My dear son," she says gently. "I got up for *fajr* prayer and thought I'd check on you. Do you want a sandwich? Tea? Biscuits? You have to eat well for your *mozakra.* If your stomach is empty, you won't be able to study! You'll forget everything before your master's exams."

"No, Mama. *Shukran.* Thanks."

She inhales sharply, her eyes widening. "You're wearing shorts? Your bones will absorb the cold air, and you'll get sick. And you forgot you have a sister in the house? *Eib teshoufak keda.* It's inappropriate to see you this way. *Eib!*"

"Asif. I'm sorry, Mama. I'll change."

"And put away your clothes. Hang them in your closet. You're thirty-four *ya* Fareed. I shouldn't be reminding you."

Fareed sighs. "I will. Just let me finish studying. My exam's tomorrow and I don't have time after work, remember?"

She looks at him with a stern face that slowly softens into a smile.

"*Mashi.* Okay. I'll come back to check on you. I'll pray for you. I always do. *Rabbena ye'lam.* God knows."

She lingers in the doorway for a moment, her eyes soft but searching, before quietly closing the door.

Fareed exhales. The silence in the room feels heavier now.

Fareed's phone vibrates. It's Eddie.

He always panics when Fareed disappears, afraid that

something's happened, that someone's found out, that Fareed's secret has slipped.

Mahitab Mahmoud

Nelly—One

Meet the alien. I'm the alien you know, or perhaps the one you don't know. I'm the alien next door, not from another planet. I'm the alien you can't help but ask where she's from, and then ask again because you don't like the answer. I'm the alien you pretend or refuse to welcome, the alien the news is obsessed with, the alien that attends to your wounds but whose wounds you never see. I'm the alien you trust with your life until you hear her accent.

That's what Nelly wrote in her journal that day. It's the journal she keeps inside her car to jot down her thoughts as she's having lunch by herself. She takes the wet wipes out of the glove compartment to wipe her hands and mouth, then she sprays the hand sanitizer over her palms. She remembers the cut in her palm when it burns. She's aware of how her OCD controls every aspect of her life. Luckily, she's a nurse. She feels comfortable at work because she has no reason to hide her obsession with hygiene.

She puts on her hoodie and looks around to see if anyone can see her. It's New York! People are too busy, running around to different destinations. She knows she's invisible until she does or says something unfamiliar. She doesn't want people to stare at her while she's praying, so the hood is perfect camouflage. She adjusts the hood to hide her face and whispers, *Allah Akbar*, God is the greatest, beginning the prayer. As she's praying, a shadow moves across her window. She freezes mid-prayer for a few seconds, eyes wide, pretending to study the tree outside. When the man walks away, she whispers the rest of the verse with a voice that is deeply shaking.

Nelly envies Fatoumata who prays at work. Fatoumata is also a nurse who immigrated from Senegal when she was young. She is unapologetically herself. In the nurses' lounge, she spreads her mat, says *Allah Akbar*, with a voice as steady as stone. Nelly feels embarrassed when she does that. She thinks that public prayer makes the stereotypes about Muslims stick. That's why she prays while sitting in her car, quietly, unseen. She assures herself that God understands.

Nelly walks back into the building, remembering she had a gynecologist appointment in the walk-in clinic during her break. It's for the intolerable menstrual pain she struggles to endure every month.

"We'll need a urine sample," says the nurse, handing her a cup.

"No need for it. I'm not pregnant," Nelly replies flatly.

The nurse answers with a polite smile, "I understand, but you still have to do it."

"You don't understand," Nelly says, lowering her voice. "I can't be pregnant..."

The nurse looks at Nelly, poker-faced.

Nelly hesitates, then whispers, "I'm a virgin."

The nurse blinks once, her face unchanged.

"Well... I still need the urine sample," she says quickly before leaving the room to end the conversation.

Nelly exhales and rolls her eyes. She's tired of explaining herself—tired of justifying how premarital sex isn't just a scandal, but a taboo, a crime and a sin for girls who come from where she comes from. It's a death sentence.

***

After the doctor's appointment, Nelly walks back to the main building and heads to Room 205. It's time for Mr. Newman's meds and vitals. Mr. Newman smiles when he sees her.

"How're you today, Mr. Newman?"

"Not so good."

"Why?"

"Because I didn't see you this morning! They sent another nurse. She's grumpy."

Nelly smiles. "I'm sorry. They needed me elsewhere, but I'll be taking care of you until you're discharged."

"Hmm. You better! The other nurse with a headscarf, what's her name? I believe it starts with an F. I don't trust her. She scared the hell out of me when I opened my eyes. You can never trust them, you know? *Them*!"

Nelly's smile fades. She wonders if he's pissed off because Fatoumata is obviously a Muslim, or because she's an immigrant, or maybe both… Sometimes she's grateful she passes as White, even though it's categorized as the "Other" on official papers, yet she can't help wondering whether that's a blessing or a curse.

"Your blood pressure is high, Mr. Newman. You need to rest."

"Everybody keeps saying I need to rest. How can I rest? Don't you watch the news?"

"I don't," she lied. "You shouldn't either. I'll come back to check on you."

"Okay, sweetie."

When she opened the door, Fatoumata was standing outside. Mr. Newman started to speak, but Nelly shut the door swiftly before he could. Fatoumata asked warmly, "Is everything alright, sister?"

"Yes, yes! He's fine. He just needs to rest."

Fatoumata had this suspicious look on her face.

"Did you check his vitals?"

"Of course!"

"Did you pray *Al-Dhuhr*, the second prayer of the day?"

Nelly's eyes narrowed. She hates it when people ask her about prayers. She used to fight her mom whenever she asked her the same question.

"I did, Fatoumata. Don't worry about me."

"Of course I worry about you! We're Muslims, and we should look after each other."

"Jeez, Fatoumata! I don't need anybody to look after me. I didn't leave my country and my family to come to a place where I'm still told what to do."

"Jeez? You said *Jeez*? Are you out of your mind? You're Muslim. Say *Allah*, not *Jeez*!"

Nelly exhales sharply and steps away. "I have to go," she muttered, leaving Fatoumata in the hallway outside Mr. Newman's door. She blames herself for mentioning her faith. She regrets it deeply, though she can't explain why. Fatoumata is not a bad person. She is actually very kind and true to herself, but Nelly can't stand how faith, intentionally or not, turns into surveillance. It awakens a buried beast she has learned to keep sedated.

As she walks toward the elevator, she nearly collides with Eliana, a fellow nurse from the NICU.

Nelly's heart plummets, like an apple pulled down by

gravity. It's the same indescribable feeling every time she sees Eliana—her short black hair, glimmering eyes, the small, shiny nose piercing, and the trace of perfume that lingers in the hallway. For a moment, Nelly's world stops.

Their eyes meet. Nelly, without realizing, freezes in place.

Eliana places her hand on Nelly's shoulder, then says with an easy smile, "Hey there!"

Nelly swallows hard. "Hi!"

"It's my lucky day," Eliana says, her tone turning playful. "Or maybe it's fate's way of making sure we meet."

Nelly doesn't know what to say. She forgets the English she's known since childhood the moment she sees Eliana. What puzzles her more is the *why*. She doesn't understand why she feels the way she does.

"What time does your shift end?" Eliana asks.

"At four," Nelly answers. "No—wait. I mean, at eight."

"Same here!" Eliana grins. "Want to grab dinner after?"

Nelly's heart skips a beat. "Um. I—well, I can't. I have plans. Someone's coming over," she says quickly.

Eliana's smile falters slightly. "Too bad."

They stood there for a moment, eyes locked.

"See you later," Eliana says softly.

"See you," Nelly murmurs.

She inhales deeply, then exhales. A smile rises to her lips, brief, uncertain, then fades, as if wiped away by a windshield wiper. She turns to watch Eliana walking down the hallway. For a moment, sorrow and regret overwhelm her.

"You good?" A familiar voice pulls her back to reality. Another nurse from NICU.

"Oh, yes. I'm fine," Nelly says.

In the elevator, she studies her reflection at the mirrorless door. A shapeless form, a featureless shadow. She remembers she forgot to write in her journal: *Meet the Alien. The unrecognizable alien. The alien who prays in hiding. Hiding in plain sight.*

Christina—One

It was a joyful Coptic Easter Sunday that Christina and Yasmine had spent at church, their voices were echoing with the hymns they'd sung earlier. Like most churches in Alexandria, this one had a warm, welcoming aura that embraced everyone who entered. The European-style arches and marble columns stood in harmony beneath the stained-glass windows—layers of history, faith, and peace shimmering together in the morning light.

Like every weekend, after attending the service, both teenagers stayed to help with the children's Sunday school activities. This time, they were preparing for a camp trip for the next day that marks the start of spring—*Sham El-Nessim*, literally "smelling the breeze." The holiday dates back to the ancient Egyptian festival *Shemu*, celebrating the renewal of life.

On this day, children, and even adults, enjoy coloring and decorating boiled eggs that they eat later with sweet brioche. Some families go picnicking in the over-crowded public parks still open to everyone—there used to be many more before privatization claimed them. Others escape to their fancy chalets along the North Coast by the glimmering Mediterranean.

"What are you doing later tonight before the vigil?" asked Yasmine as she was preparing the snacks they're taking on their trip.

Christina didn't answer. She was stacking the children's theology books in neat piles. There was a familiar smile on her face, one that Yasmine had learned to read since they were children. It was the smile Christina wore when she was thinking of someone.

"Christina, are you even listening?" she nudged her playfully with her elbow.

Christina blinked, pulled from her thoughts. "Huh? Sorry. What were you saying?"

"*Elli akhid a'alek*. Whoever's dwelling in your thoughts," Yasmine teased.

"*Mafish*. Nothing," Christina said quickly. "Just thinking about tonight's Easter vigil. Can't wait!" She cleared her throat, then added a little too casually, "Also, Nayera's supposed to call me later. She needs help with the geography homework."

"Hmm, the geography homework," Yasmine said, pausing with a small smirk that puzzled Christina. "*Mashi*, I'll buy it. But doesn't she know you're spending the day here?

That's a bit inconsiderate of her. That's our version of her Eid, you know."

"No, no, she knows. I'm the one who offered. I'll step outside when she calls. I'll be quick."

Yasmine's smile faded. "*Mashi*," she said finally. "I just don't know when you'll see her true colors."

"What colors? She's just a friend who needs help with her homework."

Yasmine laughed, but it wasn't a laugh of joy. It was a laugh of worry. Because Yasmine knew. She knew that Nayera wasn't just a friend that Christina had known since childhood. It was more than friendship. The problem was, Christina was clueless, clueless about Nayera, clueless about herself, and clueless about Yasmine.

***

Christina's phone vibrated at 11:55 p.m. She rushed outside of the church to answer. Her heart was pounding, though she told herself it was only because she was tired.

"*Alo, ezzayek*? How are you?" she asked excitedly.

"I'm good. What's that noise? It's too loud!" said Nayera, whose voice carried irritation more than concern.

"Oh, sorry! I'm at church, you know," Christina said, smiling as if the sound of hymns behind her could explain everything.

"Oh, okay. Should I call you later?"

"No, no—Now's fine," she said quickly, stepping farther from the door, unaware that Yasmine was watching her under the dim lights in the small garden between the gate and the church building.

"Tell me, how can I hel—"

Her sentence was cut short by a deafening *thud*.

The ground shook beneath her.

In an instant, Christina was thrown forward, her body slamming against the hood of the police officer's car near the gate. What followed was chaos: screams, shattering glass, and the roar of sirens that seemed to come from every direction all at once.

Yasmine's head hit the ground hard. Her ears rang. Her hand reached her head and came back with warm blood. Through the thick smoke and flying dust, she could barely see. When she finally lifted her head, she saw what she never imagined possible: the church was on fire.

People burst through the doors—some aflame, others dragging bodies behind them. The air reeked of smoke, blood, and burning cloth.

"Mama! Baba! Christina!" Yasmine screamed as loud as she could with her breaking voice, but it was as faint as a single drop of rain falling on a highway of cars.

People began rushing into the church to save whoever they could. Yasmine felt a pair of hands pulling her up.

"*Enty kwayesa?* Are you okay?" asked a hijabi woman with a terrified face.

"*Oumi ya benty.* Get up, dear. Are you hurt? Is your family inside? Don't worry, the ambulances should be here soon."

Before Yasmine could answer her, a man called out from behind the woman.

"There are people dying inside. Let's go!"

The woman helped Yasmine sit before running toward the church engulfed in flames. People raced in and out with buckets of water. Others tore down blankets and used whatever they could find to tend to the injured.

Yasmine turned her head slowly, that's when she spotted Christina by the police car. A sharp pain pierced her chest, deeper than the ache of her wounds. Two strangers were crouched beside Christina, tending to her injuries.

Yasmine called her name, but her voice was swallowed by the chaos. The dizziness grew worse—she leaned back onto the ground. Just before the world went dark, her eyes locked with Christina's, and Yasmine saw her mouth the word "Yasmine."

Mahitab Mahmoud

Nouran—One

Every time Nouran visits her childhood home in Alexandria, it feels smaller than before. The two-bedroom apartment still holds onto its early-2000s décor, the kind that once symbolized progress compared to other households of middle-class families in the city. The crystal chandelier still hangs proudly over the *sufra*, the dining table, with the thick, clear plastic cover. The *niche* still displays the untouchable Chinese plates and the tiny plastic collectibles that have gathered more dust than memories. The thick, patterned carpets no longer match the sofa, and the curtains, with the heavy golden tassels, threaten to fall by surprise at any moment. In the salon stands the elegant Black Yamaha piano that looks shiny from afar, but full of small holes like the aging *niche*. And there is the Cuckoo Clock that scares the life out of every visitor who is unaware of its existence.

It's the middle class that seemed to have been struck by an invisible earthquake—left hanging in limbo between the upper and the lower worlds, clutching to the edge of stability with their fingertips, barely surviving the high prices and the shrinking income.

Nouran drops the heavy, biweekly grocery bags onto the floor because the kitchen counter is always crowded with glass spice jars, the spice grinder, recycled containers, and the microwave. The smell of Kolkasia fills the kitchen—that familiar smell of childhood and of Ramadan evenings at her late grandmother's.

Her widowed mother begins her inspection of the groceries and pulls out the vegetables one by one.

"These tomatoes are too soft and yellow. I told you a hundred times they should be small, red and hard," she doesn't pause. "Look at the green beans! They are aging. How many times do I need to say that the beans should be firm? They should snap when you split them," she says in one long breath as if air itself were too expensive to waste.

Nouran says nothing because she's heard this thousands of times before, and because she knows her mother's monologue shouldn't be interrupted.

"When will you learn? After I die?" she looks at Nouran, waiting for guilt, not an answer. Then, before giving Nouran a chance to speak, she adds, "*Ya benty*, don't be easily fooled. I'm not going to live forever, you know?"

Nouran rolls her eyes. "Mama, you can take the money and go buy the groceries yourself next time."

If Nouran's mother were ever to write a will, it wouldn't

be about inheritance because she owns only a small ratio of the apartment—it would be a hundred-page advice notebook, filled with detailed reminders, food recipes, kitchen notes, and moral lessons about how no one but her knows what's best for her children.

***

Nouran sits with her mom in the bedroom—the room where she eats, makes her "important" daily phone calls, watches TV, and sleeps. The bed has long replaced the *sufra* and the living room. She doesn't even like having visitors. The apartment has shrunk to this one room, just like her world.

They're having hot, black tea with milk. It's the mother's night ritual that, if Nouran breaks, it will mean she has changed.

"*Tante* Anhar says *hi*," her mother begins. "I spoke with her this morning. Her daughter, Lamia, is getting married after Eid. *Masha' Allah*. God has willed it. A flawless girl, and her fiancé is a dentist. He makes a lot of money. Lucky her!" she says while keeping her eye on the TV pretending to follow the Chef's recipe.

Nouran exhales sharply. "Mama, I know what you're doing. You're not sharing this to fill the silence. You're doing it on purpose. For the millionth time, I'm *not* getting married.

And if you or one of your friends try to find me a suitor, I swear I'll embarrass all of you in public. And you know me—I'll do it, and I won't care about your image."

Her mother gasps theatrically, hand to her chest. "*Shoof ellet el adab*. Look at the lack of manners! *Ya benty*, I was just sharing the news! You never talk. You don't talk to me about your work, your friends, your roommate—"

"I have nothing to say," Nouran cuts her off. "Whatever happens at work is confidential, I can't share it. As for my friends, there's nothing new. Nothing you'd be interested in."

"*Ya benty* I was just starting a conversation with good intentions," her mother says, her voice trembling with practiced drama. "You always doubt my intentions when all I want is to see you happy."

"I understand your intentions perfectly," Nouran says. "And I *am* happy. I don't need a man to be happy."

"What about children?" her mother snaps. "*Hatgebeehom menein?* Where will they come from?"

"I don't want children," Nouran says. "I don't want to bring more miserable children to this world. We already have enough. And if I ever change my mind, I'll adopt. There are so many children who need love. Why bring more into this world?"

"Where do you get these ideas from? You'd adopt children who aren't even your blood?"

"Mama," Nouran says, standing as she reaches for her small backpack. "You know what? I'm not staying the night. I'm going back to Cairo."

Nouran walks to the door, where she had taken her shoes off before stepping onto the carpet—one of the mother's unspoken house rules. Her mother follows her.

Nouran slips the shoes on and says quietly, "*Tesbahi ala kheir*. Good night."

"Wait! What about your brother? He keeps asking about you. You still don't answer his calls or messages, and you know this infuriates him."

"He's not worried about me," Nouran answers with her hand holding the door handle. "He's just worried about his social image. He can't stand the idea of having an unmarried, uncontrollable sister, can he?"

"Don't start a war with him," her mother warns. "You need his support, and you know you won't win."

"I don't need his support," Nouran says firmly as she opens the door. "As for the war, it has already started."

The mother stares blankly, speechless, as she sees Nouran shutting the door.

On her way down the stairwell, Nouran reaches into her backpack, pulls out her ring, and slides it onto her finger.

***

Nouran opens her eyes in the dark hour before dawn in Cairo—the city of oxymorons, where chaos and peace intertwine; where pretty ugly five-story apartment buildings lean against skyscrapers; where asphalt streets run parallel to muddy alleys; where the rich grow richer, and the poor grow miserable; and where the hands of justice move selectively, depending on who has connections.

She savors the quiet before the city wakes—no traffic, no children shouting as they play soccer in the street, no neighbors scolding their kids, no street vendors calling out what they are selling—just the faint hum of the fridge in the kitchen.

She turns her head to the pillow beside her, smiles, and runs her finger across it, as though someone had just been lying there.

It's a Saturday, and she has a full day ahead, studying for her PhD and cooking. She unlocks her phone and opens the encrypted app then types: *Good morning, honey. I miss you. What time are you coming home?*

She knows she won't hear back until nine or ten in the morning.

She places the phone on her desk and goes about her morning routine—brewing her coffee, praying, checking her email, and replying to messages.

Before she knows it, it's already 10:15. Her phone screen lights up.

Good morning, habibti. I miss you, too! I'll be home in the afternoon. Can't wait to see you! Are you in Cairo already?

Nouran types back: *Yes, I came back last night. Couldn't stand staying the night there. Will explain later.*

Alright, then. I'll get ready and hit the road. No need to wait. And don't cook! Let's order something!

Nouran smiles then types: *Take care. Love you.*

A few hours later, the sound of a car driving down the ramp to the garage pulls Nouran from studying. The engine sounds familiar. She pushes the notebook aside and moves to the door. She doesn't need to look through the peephole. She already knows.

Footsteps approach—light, unhurried. Butterflies stir in Nouran's chest as her hand finds the doorknob.

"Welcome home," she says softly.

Sara smiles at Nouran as the door opens, steps inside, and closes it behind her before they kiss.

Fareed—Two

The lecture hall smells like an old box forgotten in an attic since the 1919 Revolution. The air is thick, heavy with chalk dust from a blackboard that should have been retired decades ago. Long, curved rows of wooden benches cling to rusted metal frames, creaking whenever someone shifts their weight. At the front stands the professor, in a pale brown suit, a patterned green-and-blue tie, and neatly polished leather shoes.

Fareed sits in the middle row beside Samira. Samira wears the same faded dark blue dress every day, the one with the pointed flat collar. She has worn it since the first week of freshman year. Fareed sometimes wonders if it is the only dress she owns, or if five identical copies hang neatly in her closet. He never asks.

Samira is one of the few people he trusts, maybe because she never asks him any questions either.

"*Istargil weshrab* Birell! Man up and drink Birell!"

The low, mocking voice from behind invades his thoughts. Low, familiar laughter follows. It's the same group of young men who always find new ways to mock him. Today, they've chosen a line from that old TV commercial; the one that turns a soda into a test of manhood.

Fareed freezes. He doesn't turn around.

A paper rocket lands on his notebook. Another follows, hitting his lap and sliding to the floor. He picks them both up and tucks them into his bookbag, next to two from the week before.

Samira turns in her seat, her face unreadable. She fixes her gaze on them, then tilts her head. The young men's quiet laughter fades. The professor notices her movement and pauses mid-sentence.

"The group at the back! Pay attention," the professor snaps.

"They're flirting with me," she replies instantly, loud and clear.

The hall falls silent. The three young men freeze, and so does Fareed whose cheeks are now burning red.

The professor's face reddens. "Out. All three of you. Now! This is a master's program, not a soccer gathering."

They stand, with faces twisted in a mix of anger, defeat and humiliation. The room stays silent until the squeaky door slams shut behind them.

Fareed keeps his eyes glued to the blackboard. Samira doesn't turn to Fareed.

After the lecture ends, Fareed and Samira walk together to the canteen in silence. Without warning, Samira breaks it.

"You know," she says calmly, "some predators, like hyenas, can smell fear before they even see their prey. They feed on it. And they wait for the perfect moment, when the prey is most vulnerable, to tear it apart."

Fareed glances at her, puzzled.

"The only way to survive is to turn the hunt around. Smell the predator before they smell you. Predict the attack before it comes. Sharpen your weapon knowing you may never use it because fear alone can kill them."

Fareed's breath catches. Unsure how to respond, he says, "I have to pick up Sleem from his after-school practice. I'll see you next week."

"Come prepared," she says with a warm smile. "See you."

***

Fareed waits by the school gate, standing on tiptoe to scan the crowd. The street is chaotic: clusters of students coming out of the building, parents shouting names, and street vendors shouting over the noise of car honks. Finally, Fareed spots Sleem.

"*Habibi*, how was your day?"

Sleem docsn't answer. He looks down, and his hands are

twisting the straps of his bag.

"Sleem? Is everything okay? Did something upset you?"

Sleem's voice cracks. "I'm tired of being called a girl for crying," he continues, "when I got my math test back, the same group of boys laughed at me. The teacher didn't do anything. She didn't even notice. Or maybe she did, but pretended not to. Then they continued to bully me in the soccer practice. They kept telling the coach that I'm too soft to play soccer."

He pauses to catch his breath. "I'm in middle school. I know I shouldn't be crying. I'm a man now. I should toughen up."

Fareed is stunned.

What kind of fate makes two brothers live the same humiliation on the same day? He wonders.

Why Sleem? Why him?

"Sleem, crying doesn't make you a girl. It makes you human. Never be ashamed of it. Men cry too."

"I hate being called soft, *ya* Fareed. It hurts."

Fareed feels a sharp ache in his chest.

"I know it does," he says softly. "Trust me. You're special. You're more human than most."

Fareed pauses to lighten his tone. "As for the math test score, I'll help you when we get home. We'll work on whatever you find difficult. The whole point is to learn from mistakes."

They walk home in silence. The air feels heavier than usual, but neither of them breaks it.

***

Later that evening, Fareed walks into his room, his mind drifting to Eddie and to the comfort he brings.

From the living room, he hears Sleem cheering at the soccer game he is watching with their father, followed by bursts of argument from the TV commentators and the clatter of the pots from the kitchen where Amina is preparing dinner.

Fareed closes the door quietly, pulls out his phone and calls Eddie.

"Hello beautiful. How was your day?"

"Not so well, but luckily, it's passing. Talking to you will make it better."

"What happened? Are you okay?"

"I am. Don't worry. Nothing new. How was yours?"

"It was fine. I just couldn't stop thinking about you. Imagining us both, together on a beach, holding hands and kissing."

Fareed smiles.

"One day we'll be together," he says.

"Are you planning to come out to your parents?"

Fareed frowns.

"Eddie, I cannot come out to my parents. This is not Germany. It's not an option. It's not even about acceptance of a gay child. It's—"

A familiar creak interrupts him.

It's the floorboard outside his door.

This time, it's close. Too close.

Fareed turns sharply. Radwa's eyes are fixed on him.

His hand trembles so violently that it takes him several seconds to end the call.

"*Etfooh aleik!*" She spits. Literally. "I'm telling Mama and Baba!" she yells.

She bolts out of the room before Fareed can find his voice.

Fareed's knees buckle.

He nearly loses control of his bladder.

Nelly—Two

Nelly heads to her car right after her shift ends. She opens her journal and writes what has been eating at her mind:

It runs in my blood.

It sneaks in like a snake that sinuously crawls toward its prey. It coils around my heart, squeezing slowly, mercilessly, under the sun. Then it strikes, injecting its venom through its grooved fangs without shame.

It slaughters the vessel of tears, unleashing a flood that refuses to stop.

It sucks the few happy moments I hid deep inside, the ones I thought belonged only to me.

I've become poisoned. Loneliness now runs in my blood.

My faithful enemy, my malevolent companion.

She closes the journal and turns the engine on. Before she pulls out of the parking lot, her phone rings. A video call. Mama.

Nelly hesitates, then she slides her hood on and answers.

"Mama, *ezzayek?*"

"*Alhamdulillah*, all is good. How are *you*? Do you still

pray?"

Nelly exhales. "Mama, please stop asking me that question. I do! If you keep asking, trust me, I'll eventually stop."

"*Ya benty*, I'm just concerned because you're in a foreign country all by yourself. You need God's protection. *Rabbena yehfazek*. May God keep you safe. Do you eat well?"

"Yes, Mama. I do. Again, don't worry. I won't starve."

"What about marriage? Have you changed your mind? Your cousin, Hussein, is flawless! He's—"

"Mama, please," Nelly interrupts. "I have to go. I'll be late."

"*Mashi ya benty.* Take care of yourself and eat well."

The call ends.

A heavy weight settles in Nelly's chest. The thought of marrying a man, of living that life, suffocates her.

***

Nelly drives back to Fifth Avenue in Bay Ridge, Brooklyn. Before she left for the U.S. to study nursing, her mother only had one condition for Nelly, which is to live in an Arab American neighborhood.

Fifth Avenue is home to mostly wealthy Egyptian, Yemeni, and Palestinian immigrants. This street reminds

Nelly of El-Mansheya in Alexandria, where shopkeepers display their imported goods on the sidewalks: prayer mats, rosaries, and stands of colorful head scarves and Nubian gowns. The air is heavy with incense, and Quranic verses echo from every storefront, each softly competing with the next.

What softens her heart is the call to prayer—quieter here, gentler than back home. It feels like home, a home she misses yet can't bear to return to. She wants to be unrecognized, unseen, unassociated. Some days, she wishes for an invisibility cloak like Harry Potter's, so no one would see her, and no one would see through her.

This is where she shares an apartment with her roommate, Nick. He had texted her earlier to let her know that his partner, Josh, would be coming over.

Nelly loves them both, but she's always burdened by Josh's visit because of their neighbors who can't seem to mind their own business. The fact that she shares an apartment with a man is unfathomable to them. It's a scandal disguised as a rumor waiting to spread when her neighbors know who she really is.

Nelly stops by the deli on Fifth Avenue, the one that sells the authentic Egyptian food that reminds her of the home she loves and resents equally.

She points at her favorite *batates bel lahma*, potatoes and meat, then at the mount of white rice beside it.

"Anything else?" asks the man behind the hot bar.

"No, thank you," she says.

She always speaks English here. It's easier that way. The moment they hear her Arabic, the questions begin.

"Where did you say you're from again?" he asks anyway, tilting his head.

"I never mentioned where I'm from, and I'm not planning to. Here you go." She slides her debit card towards him.

It took him a few seconds to swallow his pride before he lifted his hand to take the card.

When she leaves, she feels his gaze follow her to the door.

***

Nelly arrives at the apartment. She hugs Nick hello, and they chat for a few minutes, complaining about nosy people, about how everyone in the building seems to be listening through walls. Then she escapes to her room.

She sets her food on the desk, changes clothes, then eats in bed. She turns on a show for background noise.

Her phone vibrates. A new notification: a match on one of the dating apps she's downloaded and deleted a dozen times.

She scrolls through the profile. "He loves reading, fishing…" She laughs to herself. "*Fishing*? Is this still a thing?"

She keeps reading. "Anyway, boring!" She swipes left.

A new profile appears. This one catches her eye; a charming man whose interests seem suspiciously similar to hers. She swipes right. At the split second her finger moves across the screen, she notices the small cross tattooed on his shoulder.

She knows she's supposed to date men, if she ever plans to get married. But what if she doesn't? What if she doesn't want to marry anyone, Muslim or not?

The real reason, she knows, lies deeper. She's tired of men who look the same, think the same, love the same way. The ones who fall in love at first sight but tell her to change everything about herself.

She doesn't want to marry someone of the same race, the same culture, the same faith. She doesn't want to be mirrored. She wants to be seen and heard.

But what about women? She asks herself, then dismisses the thought in the same breath. It terrifies her.

Her phone screen lights up.

A new notification from Eliana.

Nelly's heart drops. She unlocks her phone and opens the message: *Hi Nelly. You said someone was coming over. How was it? Hope you had fun!*

Nelly smiles—a soft, unconscious smile that lingers without her realizing.

She heads to the kitchen, where Nick and Josh are cooking dinner.

"Look at that smile," Nick teases.

Nelly's smile vanishes, and a faint blush replaces it.

"I know that smile," says Josh, grinning. "It's a gay one!"

Nick and Josh burst out laughing. Nelly rolls her eyes.

"How many times do I have to tell you I'm not gay? Just because *you two* are doesn't mean everyone else is," she says.

"Girl, you're the most stubborn closeted homophobe I've ever met!" Nick says, laughing.

Nelly's face reddens. "I'm not homophobic. My best friend Maram is a lesbian. I'm *not*," she snaps.

"Okay, okay," he says, the corner of his mouth curving into a smile he fails to hide.

Nelly grabs her water bottle from the counter then heads toward her room.

"How long do you think it's gonna take her?" Josh asks Nick once she's gone.

"Hopefully sooner than getting married and having kids," Nick says.

"Poor girl," Josh murmurs.

Christina—Two

When Christina opened her eyes, everything around her was blurred. The smell of antiseptic and smoke filled the air. Then she felt a warm hand holding hers. A familiar voice, thick with tears, whispered beside her.

"Christina…"

She turned her head slowly. It was Yasmine.

"Christina!" Yasmine said with a faint smile and trembling lips.

"What happened to your head?" Christina's voice cracked as she noticed the thick white bandage wrapped around Yasmine's forehead.

"I'm okay," Yasmine said softly. "*Elmohem enty*. What's more important is you," she paused to take a deep breath. "And don't worry. Our parents were saved too. The people who rushed into the church… they carried out whoever they could. Some of the injured. Some of the…" she hesitated, "the ones they hoped were still alive."

Christina stared blankly at Yasmine.

"Where are they now?" she finally asked.

"They had to go pay before they treat our wounds," Yasmine said bitterly. "That's how much our country cares about us."

A nurse approached Yasmine from behind. "Go back to your bed," she said, frowning. "*Khatar keda.* It's dangerous. You in particular need rest."

Later that day, they learned the numbers: at least twenty people were killed, and sixty-two injured in the attack on the church. Even the nearby mosque had been damaged by the explosion.

It was everywhere on the news—the same footage looping endlessly, the same news anchors parroting the official narrative fed to them by the government:

It was a bomb planted by a terrorist group targeting our national security. We stand strong, Muslims and Christians, hand-in-hand. This will not shake us. This country is unshakable, no matter how much the rest of the world wants to see us fall.

But people had their own narratives: some said it was a suicide bombing by ISIS, others swore it was a car bomb planted by a college student who was among those who burned in the blast.

The government never addressed their questions, nor did it ease their fears. It chose silence, and everyone grew furious at that silence.

What hurt Christina more than her wounds was the *why*.

Why did this happen?

Why them?

And how did God let it happen?

***

A week later, Christina and Yasmine returned to school. They were struck by how much work had been done in their absence, as if the world had paused only for them, while moving on for everyone else.

When Christina and Yasmine arrived at the classroom door, their friends hurried to hug them, showering them with questions and relief. Everyone seemed genuinely happy to see them— everyone except one.

Nayera stayed seated, head down, pretending to copy what the teacher had written on the board.

Christina hesitated. She had always sat next to Nayera, but now Nayera's desk was three rows away. She tried to catch her eye, but Nayera didn't look up at her once.

Yasmine poked her gently from behind and whispered, "Stop looking at her. Ignore her."

She then directed Christina to two empty seats in the back. After they sat down, Christina asked quietly:

"Why? I don't understand."

Yasmine sighed, keeping her voice low. "You really don't get it, do you?"

Christina turned slightly in her seat, her body still stiff and sore from the injuries. "What is it that I'm not getting?"

"Christina!" the teacher called on her. "Face the board!"

"Sorry, Miss Hoda," she murmured, straightening up. It was the only moment Nayera allowed herself a quick glance in her direction.

When the bell finally rang and Miss Hoda left the room, Christina stood before Yasmine could stop her. She walked straight toward Nayera's desk in the front.

"Nayera, *ezzayek*?" she asked softly. "You didn't call to check on me. I thought you would."

Nayera lifted her head slowly. Her eyes met Christina's for a brief second—cold, blank, distant. It was as if she no longer recognized her.

A gentle tap on Christina's shoulder pulled her back. It was Yasmine.

"*Yalla*, we have Religion now. Ms. Sonia's waiting outside," she said quietly.

It was the usual routine. The Christian students left for their small classroom down the hall, while the Muslim students stayed behind. Two separate lessons. Two separate universes.

Christina felt an inexplicable ache rise in her chest. She

turned to Yasmine, and they walked out together. But halfway down the corridor, Christina reached out and stopped her, fingers tightening around Yasmine's wrist.

"What is it that I don't know?" she asked in a low, steady voice.

Yasmine sighed. "You know who her father is, don't you?"

"He's an imam."

"Yes," Yasmine said, glancing around her before lowering her voice, "but not just any imam. The kind of imam who's on the government's radar for extremist views. Imams don't hate us—I've heard them on TV calling for love and peace among believers, regardless of faith. Our neighbors and friends are Muslims. They show us nothing but kindness. But her father hates us. He's the one who goes on television, shamelessly denouncing our faith, saying our churches are a threat to society."

Christina froze. "What does this have to do with me and Nayera?"

Yasmine raised her eyebrows, her tone sharper now.

"It has everything to do with it. He's proud of what happened. He calls it *justice*. He celebrates it as a win. And Nayera," she paused, searching Christina's face, "she looks up to her father. That's why she only called you late at night, when he was asleep. She could never talk to you in daylight, not when he was around. But you—you were always there, even half-asleep, ready to answer."

Christina's throat tightened. "You're wrong. She's not like him. She can't be."

Yasmine looked away, her voice started to shake. "Why do you defend her so much? Have you ever asked yourself that? She's not just a friend, is she?"

Christina frowned. "What do you mean? Of course she's just a friend. What else would she be?"

Yasmine didn't respond. She just stood there, watching Christina. She couldn't throw any more hints her way. What she had already said about Nayera was enough. Christina needed time to breathe before Yasmine could tell her the rest. The other truth. The one that could either set her free or leave a scar she'd carry for life.

Nouran—Two

Nouran and Sara bought their promise rings one year after they began dating. They still remember how it all started—back when Nouran taught at a private university in Alexandria, and Sara worked there as an administrator. It didn't take long for them to become friends. Both were quietly enduring storms of their own: Sara was on a secret journey to understand who she was, and Nouran was struggling with her feelings for a colleague. Both paths were forbidden, so each of them suffered in silence.

There were demons Nouran had been fighting for years— one of them was her brother, Hisham, who, before eventually traveling abroad, seized every opportunity to control her life. She still remembers the day she decided to take off her hijab, and how he tried to throw her out of the house.

"Shame on you!" he had shouted, loud enough for the neighbors to hear. "What will I tell people? That my sister lost her faith? That we failed to raise you? Shame on you!"

"I sent you the research I found on the other interpretations of the verses so you could read," she said quietly. "I didn't just take it off, and I didn't lose my faith—"

"What research?" he barked. "Since when do we question those who know better than we do? The principles? The Qur'an?"

He spat in her face before she could reply.

Nouran left home that day and spent the night at her colleague's apartment, which wasn't a safe place either. That's where another demon waited: feelings she couldn't explain, acts of care that weren't meant for friends, and the heavy, daily work of pretending to be someone she wasn't.

She couldn't express her feelings— not because they weren't real, but because she knew they weren't returned. And, most importantly, because she couldn't trust anyone. One confession to the wrong person could mean losing her family. One confession could cost her job. One confession could mean a life sentence, or worse. Just one confession could erase her existence.

And was it worth it, when the person she loved couldn't even handle the darkness she was slipping into?

"If you were drowning and someone was clinging to you," the colleague once said, "it's only human nature to let them go so you can survive."

Nouran never knew if what the colleague said was an act of selfishness or self-care.

Sara, on the other hand, carried existential questions that

no one dared to answer—questions that stretched beyond identity, beyond faith, beyond existence itself. Questions that made people uneasy, as if merely thinking about them might summon the unknown. She often wondered whether it was fear of the questions, fear of the answers, or simply the inability to think at all.

Sara and Nouran found comfort in each other's company. There was something rare about their conversations: a sense of safety neither of them had known before. With each other, they didn't need to filter or pretend. Deep down, each knew she needed the other, though neither was fully conscious of it yet. They were still learning to navigate the harshness of their realities, and the truths quietly forming beneath their identities.

Working in the same place made it easier to connect during their lunch breaks and even after working hours, but Nouran could not stay at that university for long. She had a growing disgust with bureaucracy, favoritism, and hierarchies.

There was one professor that Nouran graded papers for, prepared lectures for, and even handled her students' exams.

One morning, that professor summoned Nouran to her overdecorated office with the leather chairs and crystal chandelier.

"How come Abdulrahman passed his exam?" she asked flatly, flipping through the papers.

"He passed because he wrote two essays that met the

highest criteria in the rubric," Nouran replied.

"Hmm, no," the professor said without making eye contact with Nouran. "He's not passing. He was absent too often, and when he did show up, he talked too much. I don't like him. The same applies to Mohamed and Sheriff."

Nouran stared at her, speechless. This was the same woman she'd once looked up to—her supposed role model, now shrinking before her eyes.

"I'm not changing their grades," Nouran said finally, her voice calm but firm.

"Excuse me? Did you just say you're *not* doing it? *Enty fakra nafsik meen*? Who do you think you are?" the professor snapped, her eyes wide with indignation.

"Yes," said Nouran. "And I know exactly who I am, which is why I'm quitting."

Nouran walked out of the professor's office and straight to the Dean's suite to hand in her notice.

"Are you sure about this, Nouran?" the Dean asked—one of the few people she knew genuinely respected her.

"Yes, Professor. I can't take this anymore. It's time to prioritize my mental health. To practice what I preach."

The Dean sighed. "Just so you know, it won't be any different anywhere else in this country. Don't have high hopes. They break necks."

***

At the Office of Worker Affairs, Nouran confirmed she was legally allowed to resign; her contract was expiring soon, and she was in no violation.

But a month later, she was served with a court notice demanding 10,000 EGP for "quitting without authorization." It sounded absurd, and it was. The notice required immediate payment or threatened confiscation of property equal in value. Nouran didn't have that kind of money at home, neither did her mother.

"*'Amalti eh*? What did you do?" her mother cried. "Your blunt, unbridled mouth must be the reason! Who did you upset?"

"Mama, please," Nouran said quietly. "Let me handle this."

Her mother crossed her arms, shaking her head. "You never listen. And look where upsetting the wrong people has gotten you!"

Nouran turned away before she could say something she'd regret later.

The government officer, who had delivered the notice, had already begun to stroll slowly around the living room, scanning everything with calculating eyes. His gaze landed on the piano.

"This must be worth a lot," he said, pointing. "The *niche*, too."

At this point, Nouran realized that she had to do what she hated the most. She called a friend who is a prosecutor. He asked her to put the government officer on the phone.

The officer froze when Nouran handed him the phone and said, "The prosecutor would like a word with you."

After a tense minute, he hung up, pale. "*Asif*," he stammered. "I didn't know who you were. I was just following the orders from my superiors. Whoever you upset has claws."

Nouran looked at him quietly. "And I have the clippers."

Fareed—Three

Radwa storms into the living room and yells, "Sleem, go to your room!"

"What?" he asks, startled.

"I said go to your room. Now!"

"Radwa, *fi eh*? What's going on? Don't yell at your brother," Zakareya says firmly.

"I need to talk to you and Mama privately. It's urgent."

Zakareya studies her for a few seconds, then exhales heavily. "Sleem, go to your room, and tell your brother dinner is almost ready."

Sleem sighs loudly and trudges toward his room.

"*Fi eh*?" asks Amina, still holding the kitchen towel in her hand. "*Ekhlasi*. Get it over with. The food will burn."

Radwa glances around to make sure Fareed and Sleem aren't within earshot, then leans closer. Her voice drops to a whisper. "Fareed is *alwan*. Colors."

Both parents stare blankly.

"I'm telling you Fareed is *alwan*!" she repeats, louder this time.

Zakareya's expression tightens. "What do you mean by *alwan*?"

Radwa swallows hard. "He's *methlee*. Gay," she says in a barely audible voice.

Zakareya's hand snaps out. The slap lands on Radwa's face before the words have fully settled. Amina screams.

"Don't you ever say anything like that about your older brother! I'll kill you!" roars Zakareya. "*Matrabbeteesh kwayes*. You weren't raised right!"

He turns to Amina. "This girl won't see the street again. No internet. Cut the cable! No TV. Nothing!"

Then he looks at Radwa, who is crying and gasping for breath. "You're not going anywhere, not even to school, until we raise you better. Shame on you!"

"*Ehda bas*. Just calm down," says Amina. "For your blood pressure."

She then turns to Radwa who knelt down with her hands pressed to her mouth. "Go to your room. *Yalla*! Come on!"

Radwa scrambled to her feet and bolted from the room like someone running for their life.

Amina gasps, then guides Zakareya toward a chair. "Sit, sit down. *Elmohem sehhetak*. What matters is your health."

Zakareya exhales heavily, his face flushed with anger. "What health *ya* Amina?" he snaps.

He stares at the floor for a long moment, then his eyes

widen as though a thought has just struck him.

"Fareed grew up," he says slowly. "He needs a wife. Find him one!"

Amina freezes, her hands gripping the back of his chair. "Now? He's not ready. No apartment. Still studying—"

"Yes, *delwa'ti*! Right now!" Zakareya interrupts her.

He catches his breath, then mutters, "There are urges—the devil's whispers. *La'nat Allah 'aleih*. May God curse him. But we must fight those urges to earn God's mercy."

Amina frowns. "What urges? Fareed has no urges. *Da zay el fol*. He's pure and good," she says defensively.

Zakareya waves a dismissive hand, and his tone hardens. "Marriage fixes men. It will fix him, too," refusing to meet Amina's eyes.

***

Fareed doesn't leave his room until his bladder forces him to. He opens the door slowly, the rusty hinges groan in protest, and pauses. The apartment is wrapped in unfamiliar silence, not the gentle, sleepy quiet of 3 a.m., but a heavy, uneasy stillness. It's only 9 pm, yet the house feels suspended, holding its breath.

He tiptoes to the bathroom then hurries back to his room. His mind spirals. Should he start packing? Will they throw him out? What will they say to the neighbors?

He sits on the edge of his bed. A storm of thoughts in his head. He then glances at Sleem, who is sleeping peacefully under a thin blanket.

Fareed wonders if he will get to see his younger brother again—if he will be there when Sleem needs him most.

He wonders, too, if Sleem will be able to face the monsters that wait for him, the ones outside their door, and maybe the ones inside.

Nelly—Three

At her desk, Nelly reads aloud what she's writing in her journal:

Many things lead to death, the most dangerous are the invisible ones. You can fight an enemy you can see, you might even win, but what about the enemy inside you?

It's not a disease you can cure. Not a pain you can dull with a pill. It's not fire you can extinguish or even the death of someone you can mourn and slowly move past. This enemy is faceless and shapeless.

Its symptoms are vapor. It surreptitiously slips into your body and soul, settling deep, then spreads bit by bit, conquering the most vulnerable places, turning your strongest parts to rot.

You start lamenting your thoughtless acts, your naivety, and the passing of your most precious time. You unconsciously lose your self-confidence, your common sense, your faith in anything good.

It turns your heart into a hollow, deserted place, and it turns your mind into that of a toddler reaching for someone safe, someone who will hold you.

Everywhere is first grey, then pitch black. You see no one. You hear no one. You begin to vanish.

Where the hell am I? Who the hell is this enemy?

The final stage: it tightens around your throat. No hand. No rope. Just pressure. Your neck squeezes, your chest locks. You choke; you suffocate.

There's no air to breathe. No voice to call out for help! Nobody understands how you're being throttled inside out.

You can't move your body. You can't move your limbs. You're paralyzed. You can't breathe... can't breathe... can't...

You're strangled.

"Jesus, Nelly!" yells Nick who was listening to Nelly reading what she's writing.

Nelly jolts, tumbling off her desk chair. "Nick! You scared the shit out of me!"

"Nelly, you need help."

"I don't need help. I need privacy! How could you stand there and listen to something so private? Did you tiptoe in here? I didn't hear a sound!"

"It's because you're depressed."

"No, I'm not."

"Yes, you are! Girl, get it together! You need help, and you need a partner."

"Seriously, Nick?" She stands and starts pushing him

toward the door. "Get out!"

"Okay, okay! Take it easy. You know I care about you, right? I really—" His voice fades as she slams the door. The silence that follows hums in her ears until her phone vibrates.

She glances at the screen. A rock settles in her chest.

"It's him," she whispers. "The charming man."

She knows she's supposed to be happy. But for some reason, she isn't.

Before she can process the feeling, the TV catches her eye.

Breaking News: Mass Shooting in Dallas. Attacker in Custody.

"Please, God. Not Muslim. Please."

She turns up the volume.

"The young man, identified as Michael Samuel, is reportedly suffering from mental health issues…"

"Phew," she exhales. "Michael means he's not Muslim."

For a moment, the room goes still.

She knows it doesn't make it less of a tragedy that the shooter is not Muslim, but it would add unwanted shame. A collective shame. A weight she'd have to carry, too.

***

Nelly has met Sam three times now. They talk about

everything from movies and travel to work and music, and she finds herself laughing more than she has in years. But she still hasn't told him she's Muslim. The word feels heavy in her mouth. She tries to hint at it instead, like tossing puzzle pieces to see what he'll make of them.

"My family doesn't know my roommate is a man," she tells him one evening. "And telling them he's gay is like speaking Chinese to them. Their brains would stop functioning after the first half of the sentence."

Sam laughs. "That bad, huh?"

"You have no idea."

She smiles, but her stomach tightens. Every word feels like a test. How far can she go without revealing herself? Now, she's bracing for the inevitable list of questions: where she's from, how her English is so good, when she moved to the States.

But Sam just smiles, not with curiosity, but with tenderness. She feels it before he even speaks. He has read between the lines. He gets it.

She asks herself: *Is that good news or bad news?*

"You know I'd never judge you, right?" he says gently. "I won't. Not ever."

Nelly exhales. How long has it been since she's felt this seen? Maybe never.

"All I care about is getting to know you," Sam continues.

"You're a book of secrets. I'm not interested in the secrets, I'm interested in the craft, the process, the outcome. The *you* inside."

Nelly smiles, but not the kind of smile that comes from the heart. It's the kind that holds back tears on the verge of breaking free. A sudden urge rises within her—to cry, to apologize, to get up and leave. To disappear.

What am I doing here? She thinks. *Do I really want this? He's not just Christian... He's a man!*

Mahitab Mahmoud

Christina—Three

It's Sunday again, but not like every Sunday. Everyone is dressed in black, standing inside what's left of the church: the fractured walls, the heavy scent of smoke still clinging to the air.

Shattered peace. Shattered faces. Shattered hope.

What eased the pain, even just slightly, was the quiet army of volunteers who showed up to help rebuild: Christina and Yasmine's classmates, their neighbors, their friends, the imams from the neighboring mosques, their parents' coworkers, even the strangers passing by who stopped to lend a hand.

Amid the rubble stood Christina, with eyes following everyone's movement, and a mind far from the present. She was grieving—grieving the loss of every soul that died that night, and grieving something else too. Someone else. Someone she thought was a close friend. Someone she trusted blindly. Someone she thought she understood.

She cried when no one was looking. She couldn't help it. She didn't know why it hurt so much, and she hated herself for it. She felt ashamed for mourning Nayera as deeply as she mourned the others.

Yasmine, on the other hand, watched her quietly. Christina's misery broke her heart. She didn't know how to help her, except by showing her the truth. But the truth was dangerous.

Christina had been avoiding deep conversations with Yasmine since their confrontation. They still talk, but not like before. When they went on a break, both walked silently toward their favorite spot in the backyard. They sat down with the sandwiches a volunteer had passed around.

"We need to talk," Yasmine said.

"About what? Me being a fool?" Christina asked. "I already know."

Yasmine shook her head. "I never said that. I just," she paused. "It hurts to watch you idolize someone who didn't deserve it. You gave her so much love and attention, and she didn't even notice."

"It wasn't love," Christina said quickly. "It was friendship."

Yasmine looked at her with a blank expression, then she said quietly, "I brought you something."

Yasmine opened her backpack, and before taking anything out, she scanned their surroundings to make sure no one was nearby. Then, she pulled out a small book wrapped in brown paper.

"My cousin brought me this from abroad," she whispered. "It's banned here—not just this book, but the whole genre. She hid it in her clothes on her last visit. Read it. It will explain your grief, and a lot of other things."

Before handing her the book, she glanced around again, then gave it to Christina.

Christina frowned. "How would politics explain my grief?"

"I never said it was political," Yasmine whispered. "Not everything that's banned is about politics. Some things are banned because they tell a truth people don't want to hear."

Yasmine fell silent when two men walked past until they were far enough away. Then she leaned closer.

"Keep the book hidden. Don't show it to anyone. Don't even mention it. The book itself isn't dangerous, where we are is. But if you read it, it'll take you to a safe place you've never been."

Christina hesitated, then slid the book into her backpack.

Later that night, behind her closed bedroom door, she unwrapped the brown paper. The title read: *When We Have No Name*.

Christina started reading, and for the first time ever, she came across the words *gay* and *lesbian*. She didn't know what they meant.

She reached for her English-Arabic dictionary, flipping through the pages. Nothing. Then she opened her laptop and typed the words into the search bar, but all she got was an error message: *Page not found.*

It was so puzzling for her. Frustrated, she continued reading, thinking that maybe the story will tell her what the dictionary couldn't.

Christina paused on a sentence that made her heart pound. She read it again, and again.

The words sounded foreign, in a language she never spoke before, yet somehow, they felt familiar. Too familiar.

She was trying hard to understand, but as she was reading, something inside her whispered: *This is about Yasmine.*

She froze.

Could she be—?

Mahitab Mahmoud

Nouran—Three

Flashbacks still linger in Nouran's mind, long after the years have passed. She remembers how she felt after quitting her job and moving to Cairo—an unfamiliar kind of relief, as if she had been holding her breath for years and had finally exhaled. Quitting freed her, and moving sealed that freedom. It was a break from the toxicity of everything that she once mistook for home: from work, from the walls that carried her brother's echoes, and from the colleague she hoped never to see again, not even by chance in a grocery store aisle.

The only downside was not seeing Sara. A couple of nights before her move, they met for coffee on a Ramadan evening. The café was glowing with a *fanous*, a lantern, in every corner, strings of lights shimmered across the ceiling, and crescent moon shapes swayed with the air.

Nouran brought Sara a birthday gift. Though the plan was to celebrate and chat about her move, Nouran secretly hoped the evening would take a different turn, that she might finally say the words she'd kept buried for months. Nouran lost her courage when she sensed that Sara was still entangled in her own search for identity. She chose to keep her feelings to herself. The feelings she wasn't even able to name. She couldn't risk misreading the moment—or worse, losing the closest friend she had.

After she moved to Cairo, they kept in touch through long messages, trading updates about their new lives. Nouran shared how she had taken out a loan to pursue her dream career. Sara wrote about her slow journey of self-discovery.

Then one night, as Nouran was reading in bed, her phone screen lit up with a message.

Sara: *Bahebbek*. I love you.

It was sudden, yet not. Nouran had heard it before reading it. It felt as though she had manifested it, as if those words had been circling between them all along, waiting for one of them to have the courage to say them.

Nouran smiled, a smile that stayed on her face for two full weeks. The same two long weeks it took her to finally open the message again and type her reply:

Bahebbek.

***

Nouran drove to Alexandria to meet Sara. It was the longest drive she'd ever taken. The happiest. She turned up her favorite pop songs, singing along and running her hand through her short hair as the road unrolled before her. The whole way, she imagined the conversations—what they'd say, how they'd laugh. She was already talking to Sara before they even met.

She finally pulled into the parking lot of the mall. Her heart was thudding with an abundance of nerves and joy. Her eyes scanned the crowd, searching relentlessly for Sara, until she felt a gentle hand on her shoulder.

She turned, and there she was—Sara, with her long hair, and that radiant, calming smile.

They hugged, but it wasn't an ordinary hug. It was the *where-have-you-been* kind of hug. The kind that heals. The therapeutic kind. The embracing kind.

Nouran's self-consciousness broke the hug too soon. Her eyes darted around, scanning the lot to make sure no one was watching, that no familiar face, no shadow of her brother, was haunting this space too.

Sara held her hand for a moment, as if she could read her thoughts.

"*Yalla*," she said softly, smiling. "Let's find a place to sit."

They walk into the mall. It was a Thursday night before a three-day weekend. Most of the cafés and restaurants were overflowing with chatter and laughter. Children ran through the wide, glossy corridors.

After weaving through the crowd, they finally found an empty table for two at Coffee Bean and Tea Leaf.

Nouran's eyes shied away whenever Sara looked at her, afraid that too much eye contact might arouse suspicion. She was still programmed to hide what her heart was holding, trained like antivirus software to block her thoughts before they could escape through her eyes.

With a teasing smile, Sara waved softly to get her attention. "Breathe," she said.

Nouran inhaled deeply, then exhaled slowly. When she looked back at Sara, it felt like seeing her for the first time—the color of her eyes, a warm milk chocolate that somehow managed to shine even in the dim light.

"It took me a year to finally text you," said Sara softly. "But it doesn't mean I wasn't thinking about you. I was just—caught up in finding myself. And in finding myself, I found you."

Nouran smiled, her eyes glistening. She wanted to stand up and hug her but couldn't.

They talked for hours, losing track of time, until it was time to leave. Nouran offered to drive Sara home.

On the way, Nouran reached for Sara's hand, lifted her palm, and kissed it gently.

Nouran and Sara return to this memory every anniversary—a flashback that softens the bitterness of reality.

Fareed—Four

Fareed wakes to the sound of Qur'an recitation echoing through the apartment, which was louder than usual, and reverberating off the walls. For a moment, he's disoriented. He overslept. It's only 10 am, but to him, that feels late. His sacred hours of solitude are gone.

It's Friday, so there are no lectures, but he knows another kind of sermon might be waiting.

The air carries the familiar scent—the sharp aroma of incense that always burns on Fridays alongside the holy verses of the Qur'an.

A gentle knock on the half-open door breaks the silence.

"*Habibi seheit*? You're up?"

Fareed stares at Amina blankly. *Is this a trap? How could she be so calm, so warm? Was last night a dream? A night terror?*

"*Yalla*," she says softly. "You need to eat breakfast before it's time for *Jumu'ah* prayer."

Fareed doesn't answer. He watches her, unsure what to read in her face.

Amina smiles a heavy, weary smile, one he's never seen before, then leaves.

At the *sufra*, Fareed can't help but stare at the elephant in the room—Radwa's empty seat.

Amina catches his eyes. "Fareed, *kol*. Eat the beans," she says quickly. "I made them the way you like them."

She continues to fill the awkward silence with the soaring prices of groceries, and her sister Rokayya's news from Kuwait—anything to fill the silence that keeps trying to speak.

Zakareya interrupts her abruptly, "I and your mother decided to find you a girl. *Lazem tekammel nos deenak.* You have to fulfill the second half of your religion."

The fork in Fareed's hand stops midair. This time the silence that follows is deafening. Even Sleem stopped chewing. The food is still resting in his mouth.

"Baba, I'm not ready for marriage."

"You're thirty-four," his father says firmly. "It's time."

He tears a piece of bread, eats it, then continues, "I'm retiring soon. The severance pay is not much, but it will cover what you need for your future apartment. Mama spoke with *khaltak*, your aunt, Shadia. She says she knows a girl—the kind every man dreams of. We're meeting her parents next Friday. You'll see her then."

Fareed feels a sharp stab in his chest. His whole body locks, heavy and unresponsive, as if struck by sudden sleep paralysis.

Amina struggles to swallow the sip of water she took, then she begins, "You know, *khaltak* Shadia kept describing how beautiful the girl is. Well-mannered and quiet like you," she smiles then adds with forced excitement, "and she cooks! A real woman."

"Where's Radwa?" Fareed asks abruptly.

No one answers.

"Where is she?"

"In her room, *yabni*," Amina says quickly. "You didn't comment on what I said about the girl."

"I'm not meeting her."

Zakareya throws his fork onto the plate with a sharp clatter. "What?"

Sleem pushes his chair back and goes quietly to his room.

"I said I'm not meeting her," says Fareed firmly. "And I also asked about Radwa. Why is she in her room?"

"*Ba'ollak eh*, I'll tell you what," Zakareya snaps. "You *will* meet her. And even if you don't, you *will* marry her, or to the girl *we* choose for you."

Zakareya stands abruptly, his chair screeching across the floor before toppling back. He doesn't say another word as he storms off toward the bathroom.

"*Leh yabni?* Why?" Amina asks urgently. "You aggravated him. Trust me, the girl is beautiful," she says softly.

"Mama…" Fareed's voice breaks. "I can't. I just can't. I'm… I'm different."

Amina's eyes widen. "No, you're not." She whispers, "There's a solution to every problem. If you need a doctor—" She pauses, sighs slowly, heavily, then says, "I can find one without anyone knowing."

His eyes fill up with tears. At this point, Fareed decides to end the conversation with, "I'm not going anywhere. *Asif.*"

He walks to his room. Amina's gaze follows him until the door closes, softly.

***

Fareed logs into the secure messaging app he uses to talk to Eddie. There are more than 20 unread messages, the last one reads:

Fareed! Where are you? I'm worried to death.

Fareed calls him.

"Hey, love. I'm okay. I'll be okay," Fareed says quietly.

"How come you're calling me at this time? Are you home alone?"

"No, I'm not. It doesn't matter anymore."

"What do you mean?" Eddie asks.

"Do you think you can still send me the invitation I need

to take to the embassy?" Fareed asks.

"You're lying! Did you finally change your mind? Something must've happened."

"Just send me the invitation, and we'll see how it goes."

Fareed paused. "I have to leave while I still have the choice."

A thought settles in: *Do I really have a choice?*

Nelly—Four

I strive to wear a smile when my inner war breaks out,

Because I can't scream out loud or even simply recount

My painful memories, my bruises, my doubt.

I fail to get what life's about.

Like an apple, hanging from a tree, I helplessly fall to the

ground.

But I've lost my mind; I'll shout!

For, of myself, I was never proud.

It's time to turn around.

I've got to mute that devilish sound

Of memories, wounds and scars to which I'm bound.

I've got to face the weaknesses and ruins inside out,

For I'm losing myself and all those around...

It's time to end my fears and doubt.

I'll neither escape nor pretend to be safe and sound.

My life's seconds may soon cease to count,

And I may find no stairs to mount

To where eternal peace is found.

So I'll turn around. I'll turn around.

Victoriously I'll hold my ground...

It's time to heal those wounds.

It's time to trust the silver line of the cloud.

That's what Nelly wrote in her journal the day she decided to talk to a Sheikh about Sam. She had spoken to her friend Maram earlier, but Maram didn't like the idea of asking the Sheikh, nor did she like the idea of *Sam* himself.

"Don't expect to hear a response different from the one you'd hear here in Egypt," said Maram. "You wouldn't get a different response from a priest either. You just met the guy. You're not even sure about this!"

"I *am* sure," said Nelly. "I guess."

"How can you *guess* you're sure?" Maram snapped. "Nelly," she exhaled, then continued, "Nelly *habibti*, you're not into men. Face it!"

"You know what, Maram? I'm gonna meet the Sheikh anyway. Let me hear what he's got to say."

"Alright," Maram sighed. "Be prepared."

It's been two weeks since she first met Sam, and now he seems to be taking the relationship seriously.

Nelly knows she can't marry a non-Muslim. Her family will disown her, if not worse. The community she grew up in would stamp her as a disgrace. She'd become an outcast, exiled by the very people who raised her.

Nelly parks outside the mosque on Fifth Avenue, gripping

the steering wheel until her knuckles pale. For a second, she thinks of driving away. But instead, she gets out and walks toward the entrance and leaves her journal in the glove compartment.

The Sheikh is waiting in a small office near the prayer hall. He greets her politely, but the moment he looks up and realizes she isn't wearing a headscarf, his gaze drops to the floor.

Nelly forces a faint smile. *Really?* she thinks. If that's his reaction to me not wearing a headscarf, how will he react to me dating a non-Muslim?

She takes a seat across from him. Awkward silence stretches between them.

"Thank you for meeting with me today, Sheikh," she says in English, though she knows he speaks Arabic.

"No problem, sister. How can I help you?"

It takes Nelly a few seconds to ask the question she has been rehearsing all the way there.

"Can I date a non-Muslim? He's a good person. He treats me better than the Muslim men I've met. And I think he's planning to propose."

"You said he's a non-Muslim?"

"Yes…"

"Is he a believer?"

She hesitates. "No. He's an atheist."

"*Astaghfiru Allah*. May God forgive me," he pauses. "You can't," he says firmly.

"Why not?"

He exhales sharply. "Interfaith marriage is clearly prohibited in the Qur'an."

She swallows hard. "How come the same rule doesn't apply to Muslim men? Why are they allowed to marry non-Muslim women?"

"To protect the wife's faith," he replies. "And her future children."

"Protect it from what? What if I don't want to have children, and I'm not planning to change my faith?"

"It's still *haram*," he replies, exhaling as though patience itself is a burden.

"I'm not convinced," she says quietly.

Then, before she can stop herself, another question slips out. "What about women?"

The Sheikh frowns. "What about them?"

"I mean," her voice trembles, "what about dating women?"

He rises from his chair, face reddening. "The meeting has ended," he snaps, his voice sharp with disgust.

He leaves the room without looking back.

Nelly sits there, frozen. She hears the *Athan*, the call for prayer. It softens her heart. She drifts into the women's prayer hall, grabs a headscarf from a low shelf, and sits.

At first, she holds it in her lap. Then she covers her head and begins to cry quietly. It's only when she feels eyes on her that she realizes a small group of women are watching from across the room. She removes the headscarf, pulls her hood over her hair, and walks out of the mosque.

Outside, beneath the dim streetlight, she pulls out her phone. As soon as her eyes catch Eliana's name on her screen, her face softens, as if the sun had risen just to dry her tears.

I didn't run into you this morning, and the nurses told me you called out. Are you okay? Eliana texts.

Nelly smiles. She types back:

I'm okay. Thank you for asking.

Nelly pauses, then types: *Does your shift end at eight tonight? In an hour?*

Eliana replies instantly:

Yes! Wanna grab dinner?

Nelly's heart lifts. She types: *I'd love to.*

Nelly then switches to FaceTime and calls Maram.

"Nelly? Are you okay? It's past midnight here—"

Nelly cuts her off. "You told me there's a therapy session you're going to tomorrow," she says quickly. "How safe is it? Can I join you virtually?"

Maram exhales softly. "Nelly, *safe* is a foreign concept here in Egypt. It doesn't exist. But yes… you can."

Christina—Four

"Don't stare at me like that! I'm not an alien," Yasmine whispered, half laughing, half serious. "You think that because I love girls, I'm abnormal?"

"*Msh 'arfa*. I don't know," Christina said teasingly, tossing a pebble toward the sea. "*You* tell me."

They sat on the massive rocks of Sidi Gaber in Alexandria, the sea stretching endlessly before them, the waves crashing against the shore, sometimes gentle, sometimes fierce.

"Christina, I gave you that book for a reason," Yasmine said, her voice softening. "It wasn't just something to read for fun. I knew it would flip a switch in your head."

"Maybe it did," Christina said, smiling faintly.

Yasmine rolled her eyes. "Jesus, maybe it burned a fuse instead," she said, laughing.

Christina hit Yasmine's shoulder with her bag. They both laughed, then the laughter faded into silence.

"No, *begad*, seriously," Yasmine said softly. "I've always felt—different. I've had friends my whole life, but there was always that one girl who wasn't like everyone else. I wanted to take care of her, surprise her with gifts, help her without her even asking. On one of my cousin's visits to Egypt, she noticed how every story I told somehow circled back to that girl. That's when she taught me the forbidden words—the words that helped me see myself clearly for the first time. It was easy for her to talk about it; she's lived her whole life abroad. But here—" she paused, her eyes drifted to the sea, "it's different. Even the *existence* of those words is forbidden."

Christina's breath caught. *This sounds too familiar*, she thought. Nayera's face flashed in her mind—the late-night calls, the gifts she bought her, the way her heart ached whenever she saw her. *But no. That couldn't be it. She's not like that. She can't be.*

"Who's the girl?" Christina asked abruptly, as if to drown the thoughts rising inside her.

Yasmine looked at her for a long moment then said, "I don't think you know her. You still don't know who she is. But one day, you will. She's beautiful inside and out."

Christina searched Yasmine's face, hoping to find something—anything that could help her make sense of what she was feeling.

"Why did you lend me that book?" she asked. "Why me?"

Yasmine took a deep breath and exhaled slowly. "Christina, have you ever asked yourself about Nayera? Do you see how your eyes glow when she walks in? Do you feel those butterflies every time she calls your name? Does that really happen between friends?"

Christina didn't answer. She wanted to say *yes*, but she couldn't. Saying yes meant she was like Yasmine.

And if they were on the same boat, they'd both drown—sooner or later.

"Christina, *min el'akhir*, to cut it short," Yasmine whispered, scanning their surroundings, "you're a lesbian, too."

Christina's eyes widened. "No. I can't be. I can't—" Her voice broke as tears spilled down her cheeks.

Yasmine's hand reached for Christina's slowly. "I know—"

"Why do you care that much if I admit it or not?" Christina snapped through her tears.

"Shush! Your voice!" Yasmine hissed, glancing around again. "Because I care about you. Living in fear *knowing* who you are is still better than living in oblivion—blind-folded, crashing into every wall, pretending to be someone you're not."

"What will I tell my family?" Christina asked, wiping her tears.

"What family? *Ya benty*, we don't say those things to families. You know what would happen if they knew?"

"I don't want to know."

"Exactly! So, keep it to yourself. You can talk to me, and to others, like us—" Yasmine's eyes softened. "We're not alone," she said quietly. "We're just silent. Silenced."

***

Later that day, Christina locks herself in her room. She is supposed to be studying for her final exams—the ones that determine which college she attends and, eventually, the kind of life she will lead. Her future hinges on a percentile.

But her mind is elsewhere, replaying Yasmine's words on a loop, like a broken record she can't turn off.

What if Yasmine is right? What if I am a lesbian? What will become of me? What will I tell my parents? What will I tell my sister?

A soft knock interrupts her thoughts. It's her sister, Marian.

"Can I come in?" Marian asks gently.

"Sure," Christina says.

Marian sits beside her on the bed.

"What's going on? You haven't been yourself lately."

"I'm… I don't know. I'm lost."

Marian smiles faintly. "Did you read the book?"

Christina's eyes widen. "What book?" She asks.

"You know what book," Marian says. "I saw it. It's okay, little sister. I already know."

Christina's heart starts racing. "What do you know? What do you mean?"

"I saw the book—you hid it in the most obvious place," Marian says with a soft laugh. "But, honestly, I didn't need to see it. I already knew."

Christina's face reddens. She says nothing.

"You know I love you no matter what," Marian continues. "I'll always be there for you. I'll fight for you—even if it means losing our own family. I'd still fight." She pauses and reaches for Christina's hand. "I knew you were into girls when Nayera came into your life. It was obvious how much you cared about her."

Christina frowns, tears filling her eyes. "How did you, and Yasmine, know when I didn't? How could I be the last to know? How could I not know myself?"

Marian squeezes her hand. "*Habibti*, sometimes the strangest stranger is ourselves. You might be good at reading everyone else, just not yourself. Your subconscious sends you hints, but if you don't learn how to read them, you stay in the dark. The good news is, once you do—or once someone helps you—you finally get to be who you are, even if it means living with limits."

Christina wipes her tears. "You're not mad at me?"

"Why would I be?" Marian asks. "Besides, you're not the only gay person I know. One of my closest friends is, and I'm grateful they trusted me with that part of themselves. They opened my eyes and helped me see you more clearly." She smiles. "I hope you learn to see yourself, too. You deserve to love and be loved. You deserve to be happy, and to make someone else happy. If that means starting a war with the world around you, then so be it. I'll make sure you don't fight it alone."

Christina smiles.

"So, how was your outing with Yasmine?" Marian asks.

"Overwhelming," Christina admits.

"I figured. But was it worth it?"

"I think so."

"You better be sure," Marian says, smiling. "I like Yasmine. Don't lose her."

"What would make me lose her?"

Marian meets Christina's gaze. "She's there for you. Be there for her, too."

Mahitab Mahmoud

Nouran—Four

Nouran and Sara now live together, work together, and share a life based on small yet meaningful rituals—a life behind closed doors. To everyone else, including their families and friends, they're simply two sister-like friends making ends meet in a city far from home. But they're not just friends. They're lovers. Partners. And secretly, wives. It was their real home.

Three years after Sara moved in, they traveled to London for a conference where Nouran was scheduled to present her research. But the trip meant more than work. Before they left, they had already arranged to meet a Sheikh, a progressive Muslim cleric who quietly officiated marriages for LGBTQ couples. He was gay himself, a man who had chosen a path that gave others like them a way to exist, to love, to be seen, even if the only way was in secret.

It was the only way they could marry. Away from Egypt, far from their families and the society that would never understand. In the government's records, they remain single. But in their hearts, they're each other's kindred spirit—home.

It was a silent kind of freedom, one that demanded love, faith, and patience to endure. A freedom that came with a price: living a double life—one as married, and another as single. It meant sacrificing the weekends and holidays, spending them with family, away from the real home.

One morning as they were getting ready to go to work, Sara asked, "How long are we going to live like this—this double life?"

It wasn't the first time she'd asked the question. And it wasn't the first time Nouran had to answer it.

"I don't know," Nouran said softly. "I wish I did. Maybe if we save enough, we can travel somewhere."

"When?" Sara pressed. "We keep saying *one day, one day*, but when is that day coming? Don't you see how evasive it is? We're chasing an illusion, Nouran. Either we create that day, or we'll never see it."

Nouran didn't answer right away. She paused, staring at the floor as if searching for an answer in the patterned maze of the carpet. She knows Sara is right, but she also knows she isn't ready. Or maybe it isn't about courage. Maybe it's something harder to name.

"What about our jobs?" Nouran asked. "I can't just leave. I can't abandon the people who've trusted me with their lives. They need me."

Sara exhaled. "*You* need *you, habibti. I* need you. And if those people truly knew you, they'd understand. And if they don't," she paused, looking away, "then maybe they were never meant to."

Nouran didn't respond. She chose silence, afraid that anything she says might come out wrong and hurt Sara further. Both are already carrying too much, the kind of burdens that leave no room for more.

She slowly slipped the ring off her finger. As always, Sara noticed.

"Nouran, keep it on," she said gently. "You're too self-conscious."

"I *am ya* Sara. I am. Aren't you, too? Aren't you worried? Am I the only one living in fear? I can't have it on in public. You know how people are—they'll start asking questions!"

"You don't have to answer them," Sara said softly. "You can also say *no*. I learned it the hard way, but it works. That ring is the only proof of our marriage."

"The only proof? We don't *need* proof. We have each other." Her voice dropped, almost to a whisper, "We *are* married. We know that. We don't need a reminder."

"I do, *ya* Nouran," Sara said anxiously. "I do need that reminder, that we're together, even out there in the world."

She hesitated, then took a quiet breath. "Nouran," she said softly in a tender voice, "I'm not going to watch from a distance today. I'm joining you," she paused, eyes searching

Nouran's. "We need to talk openly, and we'll figure something out."

Nouran froze at the door. She didn't take off the ring, but her fingers kept turning it. Every word Sara said is true and yet, she felt paralyzed. She knows Sara has always been braver, freer, more daring. Nouran's courage, on the other hand, has limits—boundaries carved deep into her soul.

She has always felt like she's tiptoeing through life, tiptoeing around people like they were made of China, easy to shatter, quick to judge. She is always too afraid they might get suspicious. In public, she feels exposed, naked, as though her clothes were transparent—not revealing her body, but her soul. Her being. Her heart.

Mahitab Mahmoud

The Odd Socks Society

Fareed doesn't remember how he found it: maybe an ad, or fate… It was a Facebook event with a title that felt too silly to be real: *The Odd Socks Society*. The post had barely a handful of likes and comments, with one phrase repeating beneath it: *the color of our names*. He later learned it wasn't just a comment; it was a code phrase shared by an underground community. Everything on social media is censored, so they had to hide in plain sight, and use codes to stay invisible to government eyes.

Fareed is first to arrive at the event.

There is a circle of chairs in the middle of the room, each with a single sticky note resting on the seat.

Fareed takes the seat closest to the window and reads the note resting on his:

Who are you when no one's watching?

He blinks, then scans the room, thinking it must be a prank, or a trap. How can the question be too intimate, too personal, as if someone had written it for him?

A few minutes later, two young men walk in, followed by

Christina and Yasmine. The girls sit beside Fareed, who offers a shy smile.

"Hey," he says, breaking the ice. "I'm Fareed."

"Hi Fareed," Yasmine replies warmly. "I'm Yasmine, and this is Christina."

"Hi," Christina says, her eyes already drifting around the room.

The room is covered in birthday decorations: a table lined with soda bottles, a cake, plastic cups, a tray of snacks, and half-melted candles. Colorful streamers and balloons hang from every corner.

"Wait," she says, frowning. "Did you bring me all the way from Alexandria for a birthday party?"

Yasmine and Fareed laugh.

"Of course not," Yasmine says. "It's camouflage," she whispers.

They exchange smiles, then fall into silence.

"I guess we're supposed to share our responses with whoever's next to us," Fareed says finally, looking at the sticky note in his hand.

"Interesting," Yasmine replies, crossing her legs. "So, what's your question?"

"*Who are you when no one's watching?*" Fareed reads aloud, then exhales.

"And?" she asks, grinning. "Who are you?"

He hesitates, then smiles. "I'm someone whose identity doesn't exist on record," he says quietly.

Yasmine chuckles. "Well, you're not alone." She winks, then says, "Same here."

The three of them let out a breathy laugh of relief.

"I never imagined I'd sit in a public place in Egypt and say *this* to two strangers I've just met," he says.

"Tell me about it!" Yasmine says, smiling.

"What about your note?" Fareed asks Yasmine.

She unfolds her note. Her smile fades. Her gaze fixes on the paper as if she's studying the features of someone in a photograph.

"Yasmine, *fi eh?*" Christina asks gently.

Yasmine hesitates, then reads: "*Who would you give your heart and soul to?*"

"And?" asks Fareed.

She glances at Christina for a few seconds, then looks back down at the note.

"I do have feelings for someone," she says quietly. "I just—I hope she'll see me one day. She already has my heart."

Christina's breath catches. Her mind races. *Wait!*

She looks at Yasmine, and notices for the very first time the softness in her voice, the flicker in her eyes, the unspoken feeling. Thoughts begin racing in her head:

Yasmine was there all along.

I'm the girl she talked to her cousin about.

I'm the one in her heart.

How could I have been so blind? So self-centered?

How did I not see the light flashing in my own eyes?

Fareed senses the silence growing heavy and turns to Christina.

"What about yours?" he asks softly, noticing how her eyes are still fixed on Yasmine.

"Uhm, mine says," she pauses, "*If you could live one day as your truest self, without consequence, what would that day look like?*"

Christina feels a deep ache in her chest—a quiet pull, like a magnet drawing her heart toward Yasmine, and an urge to cry. *What's happening to me?*

She swallows. "I'm not sure, but if there was," she pauses and clears her throat. "If there *is* someone I care about deeply," her eyes drift back to Yasmine, "I'd spend that day with them. We'd do something crazy. Maybe the craziest thing of all would be just—being ourselves."

No one speaks after that.

Christina's eyes keep chasing Yasmine's teary eyes. She's never seen her this vulnerable before.

Then the door opens.

A young woman walks in with her phone pressed to her ear. Her face looks familiar to Christina and Yasmine. They recognize her instantly.

It's Maram, one of the volunteers who brought food to the church after the explosion.

"*Estanni*. Wait," Maram says into the phone, then turns to the group.

"*Ahlan*. Hello! What a small world!"

The tension breaks. Yasmine and Christina smile.

"Pick a seat so you can pick a note," Yasmine says.

Maram chooses the empty seat beside Yasmine.

"Wait, do you know each other?" Fareed asks.

Yasmine answers, "Well, we thought we did, but it turns out we didn't." Her smile makes Maram and Christina smile too.

Maram's phone glows. A familiar voice calls out faintly: Nelly's.

"Did you get there?"

"Yes, I'm here," Maram says. "Wait, I'll read two sticky notes. The first one is for you. Let's switch to a video call."

"No no…"

"It's already done," Maram laughs.

"Damn it!" Nelly says.

"Uhm, hi everyone. I'm Nelly! Oh my God, this is so awkward," she laughs nervously.

Maram reads: "*When did you last feel seen by something greater than yourself?*"

"Let me think," Nelly pauses. "This question hit a nerve. Before yesterday, I felt like I hadn't been seen or heard in a while. Or maybe I wasn't loud enough."

"And now?" Maram asks, smiling.

"Last night I felt seen. And heard. I was myself for the very first time. I let someone guide me toward a path I didn't even know I'd been avoiding," Nelly says with an enchanted smile.

They all smile, too.

"I'm happy for you, Nelly! I'm Fareed by the way," he says warmly.

"Hi Fareed!"

Maram unfolds her sticky note: "*Who would you be if you were born somewhere else?*"

"I'd be freer, maybe?" Maram says. "But if I was born somewhere else with the same family, I don't think it would change much, you know?"

"Right. I agree," says Fareed. Yasmine and Christina nod.

The door opens. Two women walk in. One in blue. One in red.

"The one in blue is the therapist," Maram whispers. "They're both wearing rings, but I'm not sure if they are—" she pauses. "We're in Egypt. They can't be." She stops when the two women approach.

They take their seats in the circle.

"Hello everyone!" says the woman in blue with a warm smile. "Thank you for coming today. We're so glad you chose to join us. I'm Nouran, a licensed therapist, and this is Sara, my partner and office manager. Please, let's start by introducing ourselves."

One by one, voices fill the room.

"I'm Fareed. I'm an accountant, and I'm also enrolled in a master's program, so I'm still studying."

"I'm Yasmine. I recently graduated from high school."

"Hi, I'm Christina. Same here."

"Maram. I'm a translator."

The two other men introduce themselves as well.

Nouran nods. "I know some of you travelled all the way from Alexandria to be with us," she says, smiling at Yasmine, Christina and Fareed.

"I also know someone is joining us virtually from New York," she glances at Maram, whose phone screen shows Nelly's face.

"Yeah—that's me. Nelly, a nurse," comes the faint voice through the speakerphone.

Nouran smiles gently.

"Welcome, Nelly. Welcome everyone," she says.

She looks around the room, letting the silence settle before she speaks again.

Christina's hand slowly reaches for Yasmine's. Yasmine

turns toward her, and their eyes meet. Christina's fingers curl softly around hers.

"So, what brings us all together here is pain," Nouran pauses, "throbbing pain—whether spoken or unspeakable. The kind of pain that doesn't just pierce your heart, but twists your life, your identity, your very being."

Nouran's eyes slowly scan the circle.

"And the most loyal companion to that pain is fear. Fear of what's unseen. Unknown. Inevitable."

She exhales. "The question is, how much have you endured? And how much more can you? How long will you keep hiding from the pain?"

Fareed's eyes glisten. Tears slip down his cheeks.

"Before seeking acceptance from others, shouldn't we accept ourselves first? Do you accept yourself? Do you embrace your identity? How can you ever be happy when you reject who you are?"

Nouran looks at each one of them as if waiting for an answer.

"Is happiness a choice?" she finally asks. "Is the unseen truly inevitable? Is freedom a choice, or just a dream we keep envisioning?"

She takes a slow, deep breath, then says in a soft voice, "And if it *is* a choice," she pauses, and turns to Sara, "are we brave enough to make it?"

Her gaze drifts back to the group. "Set yourself free from the shackles. Break them. It's fear that weighs you down. But fear is only a mirage. It lingers ahead to scare you from the path, but if you walk toward it, it fades. Let it fade. Let the boldness of our names rise. Let the color of our names shine. One name. One being. Let us be—and let us begin."

A gentle smile lifts Nouran's face, then asks, "Who would like to begin?"

The Color of Our Names

About the Author

Mahitab Mahmoud is an author and educator whose work centers on identity, silence, queerness, and the emotional cost of living between cultures. *The Color of Our Names* is her most intimate and personal work to date. Through four intersecting lives, she writes about the weight of secrecy, the quiet defiance of self-discovery, and the courage it takes to exist authentically in societies that demand silence.

Mahitab is the author of *When Silence Shatters: A Collection of Short Stories*, a finalist for the 2025 Wishing Shelf Book Awards and recipient of multiple 5-star reviews from Readers' Favorite. Her writing explores the inner worlds of women, men, and LGBTQ+ individuals across Egypt and its diaspora, focusing on the quiet corners where oppression, identity, and longing collide. *The Color of Our Names* continues her ongoing exploration of what it means to be seen, to belong, and to survive emotionally in worlds that force you to hide.